BE BRAVE
LiTTLE
PENGUIN

ORCHARD BOOKS
First published in Great Britain in 2017 by The Watts Publishing Group
This edition first published in 2017

3 5 7 9 10 8 6 4 2

Text © Giles Andreae, 2017
Illustrations © Guy Parker-Rees, 2017

ISBN 978 1 40833 838 4

Printed and bound in China

MIX
Paper from
responsible sources
FSC® C104740
FSC
www.fsc.org

Orchard Books
An imprint of Hachette Children's Group
Part of The Watts Publishing Group Limited
Carmelite House
50 Victoria Embankment
London EC4Y 0DZ

An Hachette UK Company
www.hachette.co.uk

www.hachettechildrens.co.uk

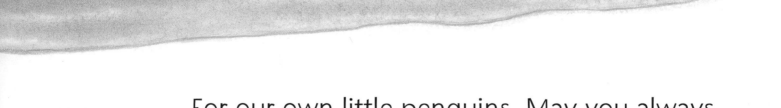

For our own little penguins. May you always
find the courage to jump! – G.A.

For my brave boys: Joe, James and Dylan – G.P.R.

BE BRAVE
LiTTLE
PENGUIN

Giles Andreae   Guy Parker-Rees

ORCHARD

In the cold Antarctic sunshine,
Where the icy ocean ends,
Lived a family of penguins,
With all their penguin friends.

There were **FAT** ones,
There were **THIN** ones,
There were penguins
SHORT and **TALL,**

But little Penguin Pip-Pip
Was the **SMALLEST** one of all.

And while the other penguins
Were out swimming wild and free,
Little Pip-Pip played alone,
Too frightened of the sea.

Names like "SCAREDY PIP-PIP"
Sometimes echoed in his ears.
He was SAD and he was LONELY,
But he couldn't show his tears.

"What's the matter, Pip-Pip?"
Said his daddy one fine day.

"You can't be scared of water!
What a silly thing to say!"

"Be gentle," said his mummy,
Taking Pip-Pip by the hand.
"We **ALL** have certain fears
That might be hard to understand.

Come on, little Pip-Pip,
Dip your toes in here, just so.
The water's calm and still now.
Do it slowly. Have a go."

"But what if it's all FREEZING?

Mummy, what if I get in

And it's just too dark and deep for me?

And what if . . . I CAN'T swim?

And what if there are MONSTERS there
Who smell me from their den,
And they slither up and EAT ME
And I'm never seen again?!"

"I understand, my darling,"
Said his mummy with a kiss.
"But Pip-Pip, what if now
You try to think of it like this …?

What if in that water
There are friends for you to meet?
And what if it is LIGHT and WARM
And full of fish to eat?"

"Take my hand, my darling.
Here, just try it and you'll see.
Please trust me, little Pip-Pip.
Come, be BRAVE now . . . just for me."

Slowly Pip-Pip made his way
Towards the water's edge.
He stared down at the ocean
From the slippery, icy ledge.

Then he looked back
at his mummy,
And, as his small
heart thumped,
He closed his eyes,
he held his breath,
And little Pip-Pip . . .

... JUMPED!

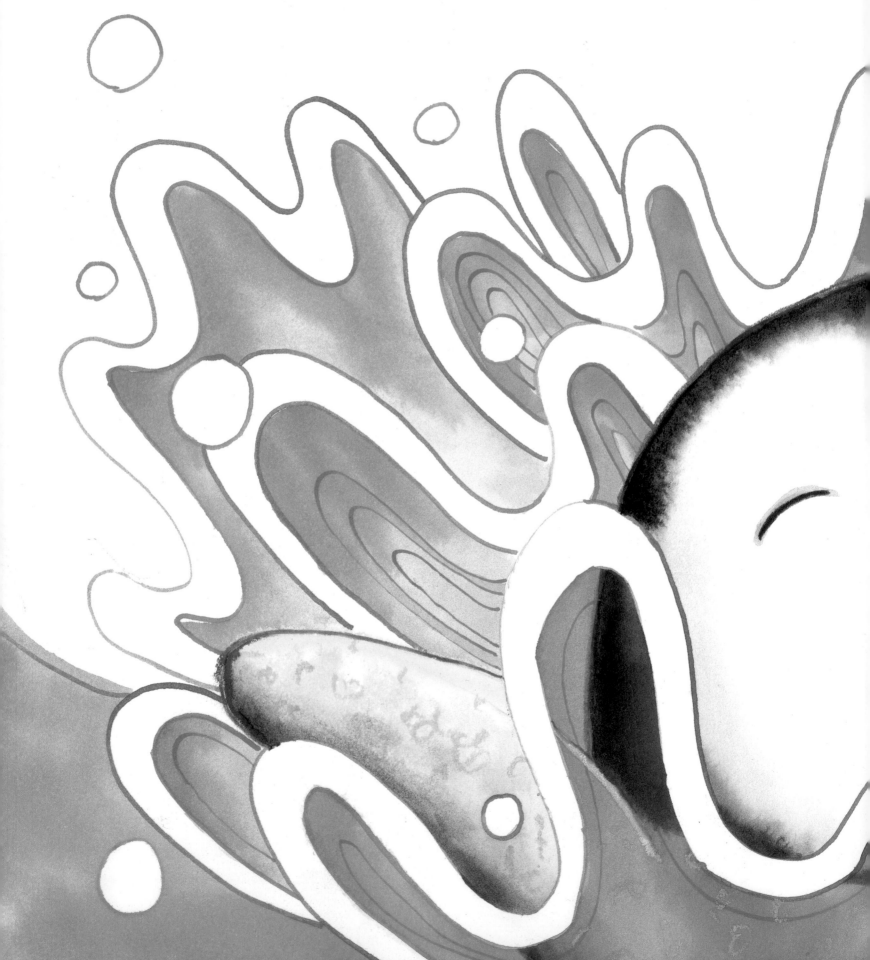

For a while, his
mummy waited.

Then she cried out,
"Something's wrong!

Pip-Pip, please,
where are you?
You've been under
way too long!"

So she leapt into the ocean,
Diving deep into the blue.

Then suddenly, from nowhere,
Came a little voice she knew.

"Mummy, Mummy, over here!
Hey, Mummy, look at me!
I'm swimming, Mummy, swimming!
Look, I'm SWIMMING!
Can you see?!"

She TURNED and, SPINNING CIRCLES
Through the water bright and clean,

Swam Pip-Pip, with the BIGGEST smile
The world has ever seen!

And, as she watched her little one,
Right there, before her eyes,
He burst up through the surface

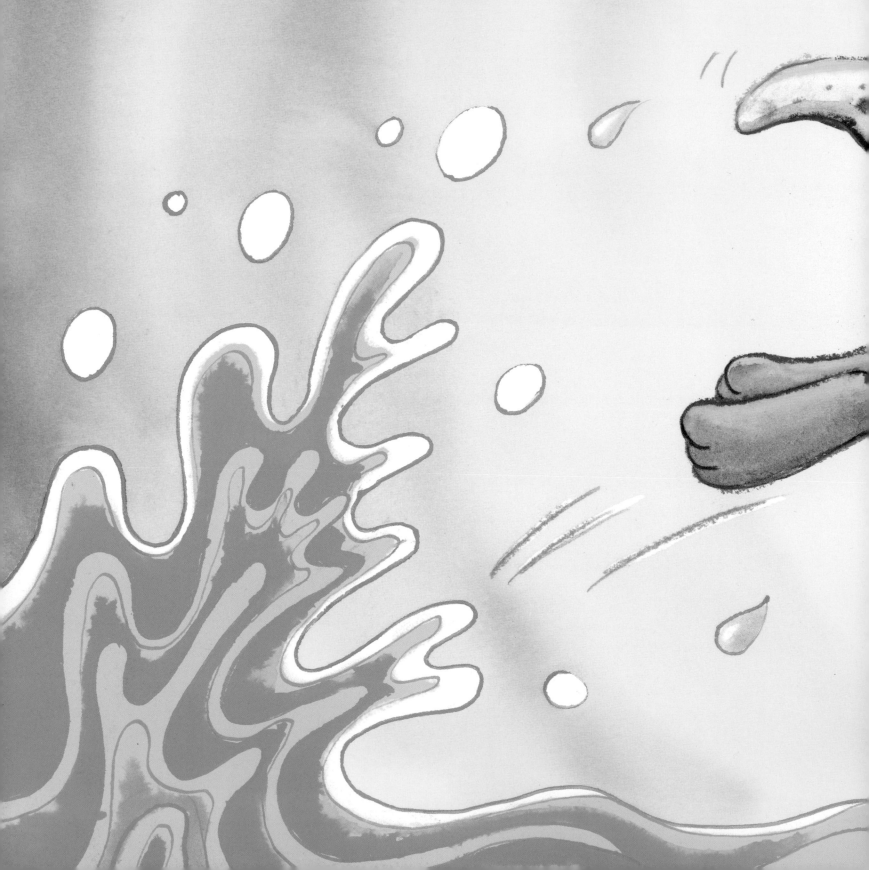

And he SOARED into the skies!

"Oh, Pip-Pip," laughed his Mummy,

As she watched him with a grin.

"I don't know about flying,

But, oh my . . . you've learnt to SWIM!"

Then his friends all gathered round
As Pip-Pip landed with a **BUMP**,

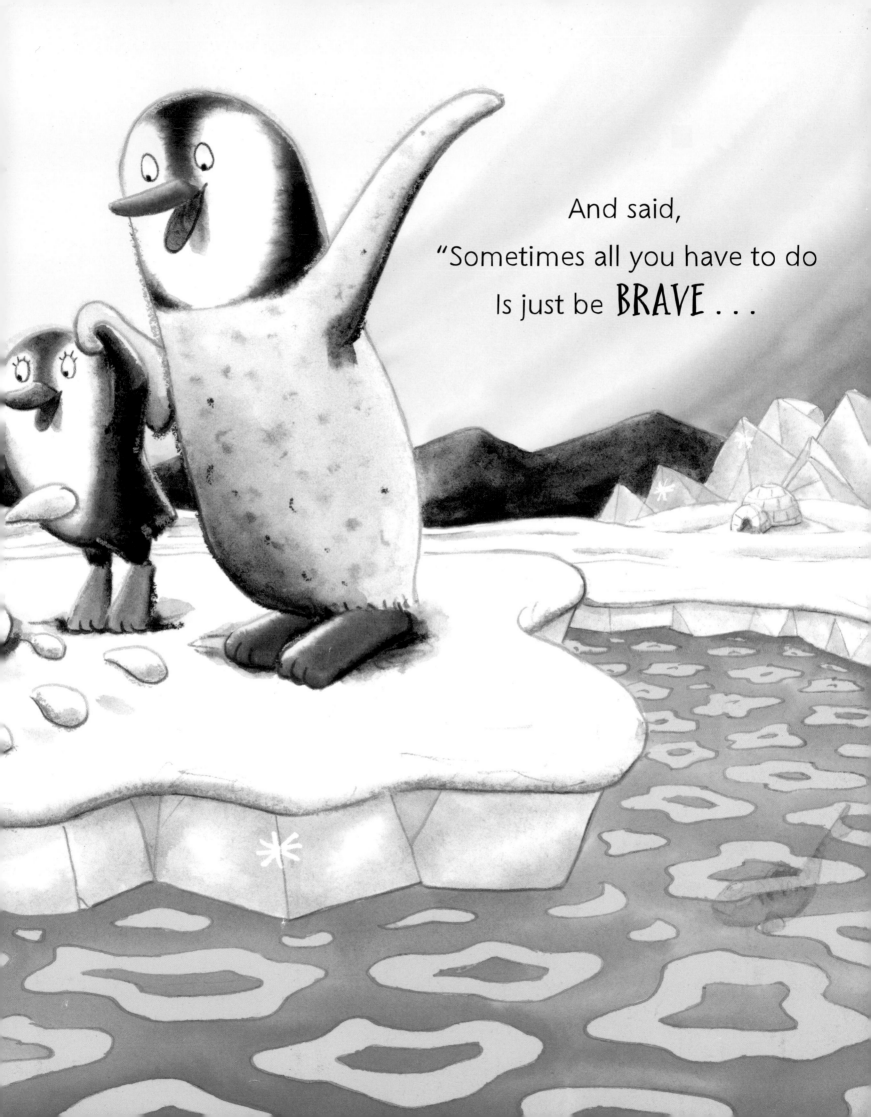

And said,
"Sometimes all you have to do
Is just be BRAVE . . .